Naughty
Nancy

First published in 2002 by
Franklin Watts
338 Euston Road
London
NW1 3BH

Franklin Watts Australia
Level 17/207 Kent Street
Sydney
NSW 2000

A CIP catalogue record for this book is available
from the British Library.

ISBN 978 0 7496 4622 6

Series Editor: Louise John
Series Advisor: Dr Barrie Wade
Cover Design: Jason Anscomb
Design: Peter Scoulding

Printed in China

Franklin Watts is a division of
Hachette Children's Books.

Naughty Nancy

by Anne Cassidy and Desideria Guicciardini

W
FRANKLIN WATTS
LONDON•SYDNEY

Norman had to look after his little sister, Nancy. She was the naughtiest girl he knew.

"I'm going out now," said Mum.
"Don't let Nancy frighten the sheep,
upset the hens, or worry the pigs!"

"Make sure she doesn't get into trouble and try to keep her clothes clean!" she added.

Norman was not happy.

Norman took Nancy outside into the garden. He showed her the trees and the flowers.

"Look at this pretty, red rose, Nancy," he said.

But Nancy was already chasing
the hens.

"No!" shouted Norman. He ran into the hen house after Nancy and caught her just in time.

Norman took Nancy to see the fishpond. He showed her the goldfish and the slimy frogs.

But Nancy wasn't looking.

She was trying to jump across the
stepping stones to the other side.

"No!" shouted Norman, splashing
into the water.

Norman caught Nancy just
in time.

He also caught some fish and a slimy frog!

Norman was wet and fed up. "Let's go into the sunshine and play hide-and-seek in the meadow," he said to Nancy.

Norman counted slowly to one hundred. But Nancy wasn't playing.

Nancy was trying to count
the sheep. The sheep weren't
pleased at all.

Norman ran after Nancy and tried
to catch her. But he just got in the
way!

Norman took Nancy for a long walk in the woods. He took his nature book with him and showed her a beautiful, blue butterfly. But Nancy wasn't looking.

Nancy wanted to catch her own butterfly and climbed up a tree.

"No!" shouted Norman and climbed up the tree after her.

But Nancy had jumped down.

Norman wasn't so lucky.

The branch broke, he fell to the
ground and landed in a bush!

On the way home, Norman and
Nancy passed the pig huts.
Nancy wanted to look inside.
She opened the gate.

Norman tried to close the gate but, too late, the pigs came trotting out!

They pushed past Norman and he fell in the mud.

"I've had enough!" shouted Norman. "We're going straight home."

And he marched Nancy back
to the house.

Mum was very pleased.

"What a good girl you are, Nancy.
Your clothes are clean and your
hair is tidy."

"What a shame about your brother!" she added.

"In future, I think I'll call him naughty Norman!"

Hopscotch has been specially designed to fit the requirements of the National Literacy Strategy. It offers real books by top authors and illustrators for children developing their reading skills. There are 43 Hopscotch stories to choose from:

* hardback